HAPPILY EVER AFTER

# Magical Creatures

KATE RIGGS

CREATIVE ● EDUCATION

# COPYRIGHT

Published by Creative Education
P.O. Box 227, Mankato, Minnesota 56002
Creative Education is an imprint of
**The Creative Company**
www.thecreativecompany.us

Design by Stephanie Blumenthal
Production by Christine Vanderbeek
Art direction by Rita Marshall
Printed in the United States of America

Photographs by Alamy (AF archive, Lebrecht Music and Arts Photo Library), Bigstock (shooarts), Corbis (images.com), Dover Publications Inc. (120 Great Fairy Paintings; 1565 Spot Illustrations and Motifs; Imps, Elves, Fairies & Goblins), Dreamstime (Sanja Baljkas), Getty Images (Apic, John Bauer, Heinrich Schlitt), Graphic Frames (Agile Rabbit Editions), Shutterstock (Darla Hallmark)

Library of Congress Cataloging-in-Publication Data
Riggs, Kate.
Magical creatures / by Kate Riggs.
p. cm. — (Happily ever after)
Summary: A primer of the familiar fairy-tale characters of magical creatures, from the various forms they take to the tricks they play, plus famous stories and movies in which they have appeared.
Includes index.
ISBN 978-1-60818-242-8
1. Animals, Mythical—Juvenile literature. 2. Monsters—Juvenile literature. 3. Animals—Folklore. I. Title.

GR820.R54 2013
398.24'5—dc23     2011050869

First edition
9 8 7 6 5 4 3 2 1

# TABLE OF CONTENTS

*"Once upon a time,
there was an **ogre** who lived in a
castle. Nearby lived a mean dwarf."*

Ogres and dwarves are creatures
you can find in fairy tales.
A fairy tale is a story about
magical people and places.

Ogres and dwarves are not the only magical creatures. Trolls, fairies, elves, and giants also appear in fairy tales. Animals that can talk are also magical creatures.

Some magical creatures are usually evil. Most ogres are mean. They even like to eat children! Fairies, dwarves, giants, elves, and other creatures can be friendly or mean.

Mean magical creatures cause trouble for other characters. But kind creatures help the main character of the fairy tale. Magical creatures can be friends or enemies.

A troll that lives under a bridge might not let people cross it. An ogre that lives in a castle might play tricks on people. But a friendly giant may protect someone in trouble. Or a fairy could cast a spell to help someone.

Sometimes a character such as a princess asks a magical creature for help. Or a talking animal becomes friends with a princess and turns into a prince!

**P**uss in Boots is a story about a talking cat that helps his **master**. The cat visits an ogre that lives in a castle. He tricks the ogre into changing into a mouse. Then the cat eats the mouse!

The Disney movie *Snow White* is about a princess who runs away from her **wicked** stepmother. Snow White lives with seven dwarf brothers. She makes friends with all the animals in the woods.

A magical creature can help people find happiness in the end.

*"A family of elves fought the dwarf and the ogre. They made the castle safe for a king to live in. And everyone lived happily ever after."*

*Copy this short story onto a sheet of paper.*
*Then fill in the blanks with your own words!*

Once upon a time, a troll named _____ lived

_____. The troll did not like people. He tried to

_____ anyone who came near. One day, Princess _____

came to the bridge. She tried to _____ it. But the

troll said, "_____!" The princess called on _____ for

help. The _____ changed the troll into a _____. The

princess went _____ and lived happily ever after.

## GLOSSARY

**dwarf**—a creature who looks like a short person and lives in the mountains or woods

**master**—the owner of an animal

**ogre**—a giant that eats people

**wicked**—bad or evil

## READ MORE

Braun, Eric. *The Truth about Ogres*. Mankato, Minn.: Picture Window Books, 2011.

Gardner, Sally. *The Fairy Tale Catalog: Everything You Need to Make a Fairy Tale*. San Francisco: Chronicle Books, 2001.

## WEB SITES

### The Princess and the Frog Coloring Pages
*http://printables4kids.com/princess-and-the-frog-movie-coloring-pages/*
Print and color pages about a princess and a magical frog.

### Shrek.com: Games
*http://www.shrek.com/*
Make Shrek roar, and play other games with this friendly ogre.

## INDEX